Our Christmas Play

Kathy Weston

Illustrated by Amelia Rosato

OXFORD
UNIVERSITY PRESS

One morning, just after half-term, Mrs Johnson said that we were going to have a Nativity play at school.

All the girls wanted to be Mary. But Mrs Johnson said that there could only be one, and she picked Rebecca.

FORDINGBRIDGE LIBRARY TEL: 652639   RIN/ree

27. DEC 00   -8 JAN 2010

02. JAN 02   1 4 DEC 2010

31. DEC 02   -4 JAN 2012

30. DEC 03   2 6 JAN 2012

22 DEC 2004   2 1 DEC 2012   Withdrawn

-3 JAN 2006   1 3 DEC 2013

22 DEC 2006   3 1 DEC 2013

15 JAN 2008

CO32 124 847 WESTON

C032124847

This book is due for return on or before the last date shown
above: it may, subject to the book not being reserved by
another reader, be renewed by personal application, post, or
telephone, quoting this date and details of the book.

HAMPSHIRE COUNTY COUNCIL

County Library

♲ 100%
recycled paper

For my family, and families everywhere   K.W.
For Louisa and Emma   A.R.

OXFORD
UNIVERSITY PRESS

Great Clarendon Street, Oxford OX2 6DP

Oxford University Press is a department of the University of Oxford.
It furthers the University's objective of excellence in research, scholarship,
and education by publishing worldwide in

Oxford   New York

Athens Auckland Bangkok Bogotá Buenos Aires Calcutta
Cape Town Chennai Dar es Salaam Delhi Florence Hong Kong Istanbul
Karachi Kuala Lumpur Madrid Melbourne Mexico City Mumbai
Nairobi Paris São Paulo Singapore Taipei Tokyo Toronto Warsaw

with associated companies in Berlin Ibadan

Oxford is a registered trade mark of Oxford University Press
in the UK and in certain other countries

Text copyright © Kathy Weston 1999
Illustrations copyright © Amelia Rosato 1999

The moral rights of the author and artist have been asserted

First published 1999

All rights reserved. No part of this publication may be reproduced,
stored in a retrieval system, or transmitted, in any form or by any means,
without the prior permission in writing of Oxford University Press.
Within the UK, exceptions are allowed in respect of any fair
dealing for the purpose of research or private study, or criticism or
review, as permitted under the Copyright, Designs and Patents Act 1988,
or in the case of reprographic reproduction in accordance with
the terms of the licences issued by the Copyright Licensing Agency.
Enquiries concerning reproduction outside these terms and in other
countries should be sent to the Rights Department, Oxford University Press,
at the address above.

This book is sold subject to the condition that it shall not, by way of trade or
otherwise, be lent, re-sold, hired out or otherwise circulated without the
publisher's prior consent in any form of binding or cover other than that in
which it is published and without a similar condition including this condition
being imposed on the subsequent purchaser.

British Library Cataloguing in Publication Data available

ISBN 0–19–279047–1(Hardback)
ISBN 0–19–272386–3 (Paperback)

Printed in Hong Kong

HAMPSHIRE COUNTY LIBRARY	
C032 124 847	
Peters	17-Jan-00
JF	£9.99
0192790471	

RINGWOOD	JATE
NEW MILTON	
FORDINGBRIDGE	2/∞
MOBILE 9	

She said it was nice because Rebecca is a name from
the Bible, like Mary, but I think she was picked because
she's pretty.

Rachel Batty *really* wanted to be Mary but she had to be a sheep. My mum told me that Rachel is a Bible name as well.

Rachel said, 'It's not fair. And I'm not going to be a stupid sheep—so there!'

Mrs Johnson said, 'No need to be rude, Rachel.'

Rebecca didn't say anything. She just smiled and pretended to rock Baby Jesus. Then Rachel grabbed the baby and Rebecca wouldn't let go. Jesus's leg came off.

Rebecca said, 'Look, Mrs Johnson. Look what she's done. She shouldn't be in the play at all!'

Mrs Johnson said, 'That's quite enough,' and took Rachel to the quiet corner to talk to her nicely.

My best friend Patrick is Joseph. He doesn't like
Rebecca, especially after what she did at his party.
He said to me that he was definitely not going to kiss her.
Mrs Johnson heard him and said, 'Thank you, Patrick, but
that won't be necessary. Now, can we *please* get on.'

Mrs Johnson said that no one is more important than
anyone else, and that it doesn't matter if you are a
sheep or an angel. But I don't think that's true.
The Wise Men must be more important than the pages
because the pages are only their servants and carry
things for them.

Nicholas, William, and Rupert are the Three Wise Men, but Mrs Johnson said that if William's behaviour doesn't improve she might have to look for someone else. She said that there are plenty of people who would love the chance to be a Wise Man.

Jessica thinks she is *extremely* important because she was picked to be the Angel Gabriel. She goes round saying, 'Be not afraid,' but no one is afraid of her anyway. She thinks she can boss all the other angels, just because her tinsel is gold and theirs is only silver and she has a higher box to stand on.

Mrs Johnson said, 'That will do, Jessica. If there is any bossing to be done, then I will do it.'

The shepherds are Louis, Imran, and Emily. They should all have been boys really, but there aren't enough things for the girls to be, and there are too many sheep already. I don't think there can have been many girls around when Jesus was born.

Anyway, you can't tell that Emily is a girl because she has a tea towel on her head.

We've all been practising very hard, because people keep forgetting what they have to say and where they have to stand. But yesterday afternoon, Mrs Johnson said to Mrs Walker, 'Well, we're as ready as we'll ever be.'

So we did our play.

Lots of mums, some dads, and some grannies came to watch us.

Before we started we all had to go to the toilet, especially the sheep, because a lot of them were from the baby class, and Mrs Johnson said, 'We don't want wet sheep all over the place, do we?'

Mary and Joseph came in first. Mary should have been riding on a donkey. But Harry, who was the donkey, saw his dad and got shy. He wouldn't come out.

Rebecca said, 'It's not fair, I shouldn't have to walk. I'm having a baby.'

Everyone laughed. I thought it was a shame because Harry was a good donkey and his dad had taken the day off work especially and was standing on a chair with his camcorder.

When the Angel Gabriel had to spread her wings and say, 'Be not afraid,' she hit Katie Potts in the face. Katie pushed her and Jessica fell off her box. Serve her right for being so bossy.

Her mum ran right onto the stage, even though she hadn't hurt herself. I'd be really embarrassed if my mum did that.

We all sang 'Away in a Manger', 'We Three Kings' and 'We Wish You a Merry Christmas'. Hugo sings really funny and Mrs Johnson said perhaps he could sing quietly. But he didn't, he sang really loudly, even when Patrick poked him.

At the end everyone clapped and some of the grannies cried a bit. Charlotte was crying too because she had wet her knickers.

Mrs Johnson said it could happen to anyone and that it had all gone very well in the end – considering. She said she was sure we'd do the play even better tomorrow.

I think we will, because this morning Mrs Johnson said that Rebecca couldn't come to school today. She has chicken-pox and perhaps that's why she was so grumpy.

I don't know about that, but I'm really glad that Rachel is going to be Mary now.

And me? Well, I'm the Star. That's because I can keep very still and I don't talk all the time.

Well, anyway, that's what Mrs Johnson said.